Then Eat My Love

Ann Iverson

Then Eat My Love

stories

Ann Iverson

Then Eat My Love

Ann Iverson

First Edition

Author: Ann Iverson
Editor: Paul Gilliland
Formatting: Southern Arizona Press
Cover Artwork: Heart by Tatjana Zlatkovic, Stocksy United
Internal Artwork: Pixabay

Published by Southern Arizona Press
Sierra Vista, Arizona 85635
www.SouthernArizonaPress.com

ISBN: 978-1-960038-15-9

Creative Non-fiction

for my parents and my past of loving and living

Contents

A Milkman and His Wife

At lunch, I asked my mother how much she could see: nothing in one eye except a circular light that floated above the retina. "The shape used to be oblong," she'd laugh. The vision of the other was dark. I wrote the check out, and she signed her name way above the line. While shopping from another aisle, I watched her use a magnifying glass to read the inch-high prices at the secondhand store. She bought warmup outfits to keep her warm at night, all in bright magenta hues; she must have had twenty or thirty. "I just can't keep warm at night," she'd explain. I suggested an electric blanket. She'd laugh again and said that she heard on talk radio that they can cause cancer. She asked me to check over another sweatsuit for rips and worn spots, then proudly told me that the nurse who gives her radiation always comments on her pretty jogging suits.

It all goes back to that fudge, those huge plates of homemade fudge. It never hardened, so we'd stand around the kitchen counter and spoon it into our mouths. She'd say, "That's why I have diabetes now, from that and the bridge mix from Woolworths. Sugar's price is high; my mother was cold and going blind. I remember sucking on a piece of that fudge while I watched *That Girl,* my mother calling up from the basement where she worked the wringer washer, "Get busy on the housework and don't run that vacuum just around in circles; get into the corners good." So, I'd turn the vacuum on and sit back down on the couch, thinking she would never know the difference. I remember that bridge mix in its white waxed bag tucked away in my mother's purse. I'd bite into several pieces until I found a malted milk ball, the only kind I liked.

My father had a sweet tooth too. He used to try his hand at baking from time to time. Once he made a peach pie but never peeled the peaches. We ate the furry thing anyway and said that it was good. He was proud and forced us to have seconds. We were disgusted by it, whispered under our breaths, "Gross, Daddy left the fur on." What a funny thing to stay with me all these years, but I'm so much like my father now, always in a hurry to get things done, rarely peeling back the skin of each day. In his retirement, he cooked noodle hot dishes, my mother would tell me, "in amounts enough for an army." He used to stop by with bags of groceries and clipped coupons for tuna at nineteen cents a can or oranges for thirty cents a dozen. "Mama and I don't eat oranges too much, so you go ahead and take these, Baby. It's a good deal." He would take his grandsons to the park or drive his granddaughter to ballet lessons, maybe even wait out in the car and drink coffee for an hour while she danced. He would revel over simple Christmas gifts like stretch gloves and a new ice-scraper, would pass the word on to my mother to tell me how much he liked those handy gloves he could just roll up in a ball and stick in his pocket. He had mellowed, ripened, closer to a fruit that I could pick and shine on my sleeve.

During my separation, I stayed with my parents for a week. In the middle of the night, I could hear him banging and clanging around in the kitchen, pacing the hallway with stomping feet. I could never figure out what he was doing. My mother explained that he would boil his coffee in the wee hours of the morning, his internal alarm still set for a milkman's hours. In the morning he would sternly insist, "You better eat something; you're too skinny. I don't think I've seen you eat a thing," as he handed me a plate of eggs. He would sip his coffee and watch me eat and tell me that I looked tired and that maybe I should just "eat crow" and go back to my husband. As a child, I was frighted by his gruffness. I clearly recall the days of him limping frantically about with huge, bulging purple cramps from years of hauling heavy glass bottles of milk, heavy glass bottles of milk through snow, heat, rain, and heat. With his hands, he'd lean against the walls moaning and swearing. I remember wanting to help, but I didn't know how. I always thought he was mad at me. But he wasn't. I know that now. He was just tired after 30 years of rising way before the sun so the world could break open with dairy. And what did I know, what did I know of the austere agencies of love?

It's easy to remember the times that he would bring home crates filled with chocolate milk, ice cream, cottage cheese. In the odd hours of the night, very much unplanned, he home from a night shift, me home from a late date, we'd meet there in the kitchen, him sitting by the window taking long drags from his cigarette, drinking coffee, and sighing big, lonely sighs. He would motion to the fridge, and I would stand with the refrigerator door wide open and guzzle chocolate milk and eat ice cream straight from the carton. "Shut that door now; that uses up energy, you know," shaking his head in disgust, our conversation quiet and distant. "Jesus, I'm exhausted, Baby." I would nod my head as if I understood, as if I could even comprehend his labored, worn-out body. "That's pretty good stuff, ain't it? There's some cottage cheese in there too. I hate to see that go to waste down on the dock, so I like to bring it home for you and Mama. Well, I'm gonna hit the hay. Say, you stick around now tomorrow. I'm gonna be needing your help in the garden." But I already have plans, I thought. Then I'd listen to him crawl slowly up the stairs to his bedroom in the attic.

I wish those times back for the chance to redo my part, to say my lines with more clarity, to remember his gentleness more than anything else. It's like that recurring dream I had as a child. I would float up and hover like a hummingbird over my bed, float down the stairs, through the basement, and hover again in the deepest, darkest corner of the cellar. Mostly, I dreamt that I floated safely and softly back to bed. But there were those nights that I would dream that I awoke in the basement, unable to move, paralyzed from head to toe in that dungeon of dungeons, where centipedes and water bugs lurked, home of the wringer washer, where my father whitewashed only half the stone. Then, suddenly, movement would be retrieved, and in my dream, I would fly up the stairs in total horror as though some snarling monster clawed at my heels. The dream would fade, I not knowing if I ever made it back to bed.

It's so hard to forget the harshness of that dream yet so easy for me to remember only the good: him bringing my mother bismarks and coffee, driving her to antique shoes, overly protecting her in her illness, making sure someone always held her arm. It would be easiest to remember them sleeping in separate bedrooms, the fighting. But when I called my mother on the phone, she would say "I am listening to the radio pretending to dance," then reminisced of the night they met at the Prom Ballroom. "Daddy was pretty light on his feet; you marry a man who likes to dance." So that's what I'll do; I will. I will remember them dancing.

Waves and Wet Kisses

I had only seen them kiss twice in my life. The first time I was seven or so. It was after my father's ear surgery. When he was young, he was a lifeguard and dove too deeply into the water, damaging his eardrums. Or it could have been when he tore the cartilage around his ribs from lifting crates of milk. I don't really recall. He wore a bandage around his torso and was off work for a while. I've always thought that he broke his ribs, so I called to find out for sure what had happened. I talked to my mother and could hear my dad saying in the background, "Tell her not to write any stories about me." But then the memories began to flow, like waves they came in, pushing them together, pulling them apart. They began to laugh and talk of the days of my father's milk route: the time he crawled on his belly to a house so he wouldn't fall through ten feet of snow; the time a woman answered the door, nude under her transparent, unbuttoned negligee; the time the river flooded and my father waded through four feet of water. And for those fleeting moments, the two of them drifted as one.

The second time was just after my mother's mastectomy. They slowly rolled her out of the operating room. She looked sad without her glasses on. Her eyes were small and watery. The sheet lay flat over the hollow home the breast had left. As the nurse wheeled her by, my father bent over and touched his lips to hers, then turned away and shook his head. Before my family knew that it was cancer, my dad called and asked, "Have you talked to Mama? I think she's sick. I think they've found a lump in her breast. You know she never tells me anything." Then he hung up. I was with my mother at the clinic when the test results came in. We waited nervously for the doctor. He sat down quietly. "I'm afraid it's malignant, but it hasn't spread." With his hand he touched her breast lightly, circling with his finger where the tumor was. Sweetly, my mother blushed but was frozen solid in her chair. And I wondered if my father had ever touched her like that. When we left the office, my mother joked, "He's a handsome duck." I laughed and agreed. Then she insisted on giving me ten dollars for gas. I tried to refuse but she said, "No, you take it." So, the breast was removed. My sisters cried. At first, if I would stop over to their house, in the morning or night, she'd come to the door in her robe. I would try not to look at the vacant space where the material hung sadly. She tried to make it seem that the absence didn't bother her, but I knew that it must have. And I wondered if it hurt my father too. I tried hard to remember another time when they had kissed. But two it is. That is it. That is all. Two small kisses for me to coast on like a wave, for me to hope on, for me to believe in, that two kisses could wash up some forgotten, buried love that they might ride the same high wave to the faraway shores of Heaven.

Chocolates

Many a moon ago my father stopped by bringing me chocolates from K-Mart. "A little treat for you," he said, "Got them on sale for a buck, pretty good deal, pretty good bargain." I smiled at him for our frugal tendencies. He followed me into the kitchen and made small talk while I heated up the coffee. He told me of his latest project of pounding out the dents in his station wagon, thought he could get the rust spots out himself, and worked on the car for three hours that morning. I looked out the window and approved his work, but he insisted that I go out to the street for a real examination. I walked to the car as he watched me from the porch. I exaggerated my enthusiasm for the blue spots where the rust had been removed. When I returned to the house, I praised him for his hard work and told him it was a big job. He felt proud; I could tell. He adjusted his belt and straightened his glasses.

In the kitchen, I poured him a cup of coffee and opened the chocolates and began to eat them right away. He leaned against the counter, pleased that I was eating the candy. He said, "You like those, don't you?" I nodded and realized that I was making him feel needed just by eating a chocolate. He glanced me over sideways from the inside of his glasses, probably thinking that I looked too thin, then rambled on about the rust spots, and I thought about him in the aisle of K-Mart picking out the chocolates. I knew for sure then that he thought about me. We went on making small talk. We tried hard to look each other in the eyes as we spoke, but it was easier to look away. But as I snuck a glance at him, I saw a grandpa. He was a grandpa. He was my father but he was a grandpa. He walked more slowly and always wore brown. But his hair was not grey and his wit was still spry. He still noticed my clean house and had funny things to say to the dog and cat. His belly was so round, I felt the urge to pat it. Before we ever really felt comfortable, we ran out of things to say. He walked to the door saying, "Well, I better be hittin' the road. Just thought I'd stop by to kill some time. Mother likes to get me out of the house, you know." He leaned one more time with his arms against the porch. I looked at those arms of his. They seemed so familiar, looked so much like mine, but I don't think I've ever touched them. I wondered if we had held the same things away. We've held each other away. I do know that. I know that now because his ten-minute visits caused me ten pages of words; his bringing of chocolates left me lonely. And as he drove away, I wanted to chase him down the street and call out, "I love you and thank you for the chocolates." But I was thin, Father, skinny of the heart. All along I had held in my mouth what my diet had lacked, and, for years I had been filling up on that empty space named fear.

Graveyards of the Heart

It was four months after my mother's death when the marker was finally set. We sat around the kitchen table choosing the right stone to mark her life as though we were picking out wallpaper. My father served us hot tea, and we "oohed" and "aahed" over the magnificence of the grand and elaborate coliseums in the catalog. We thumbed through the pages until we came to the humble, tiny stones, the meek, inexpensive markers for the little nobodies of the world, small emblems that cascade into the American landscape in droves, filling up the land, earmarking every family's loss almost identically: pale gray marble, square, and offset with scrolling flowers and a crucifix. I think we actually thought that my mother's stone would be unique, with the way the salesman dabbled over his sketches of the plot, asking for the correct spellings and dates, erasing, and sketching again, going over and over his lines with the pencil, all in nervous gestures.

My father ordered a double plot; unfortunately, it was not large enough for him to rest beside her. With all the land in the world, there was no space left for him to sleep beside his bride. In a little Catholic cemetery, she bears a single plot, beyond a small lake, in a row of unfamiliar, identical losses, rows and rows and rows of grievance all lined up neatly, as though tidiness could even be a part of it.

I pondered the dead, who they were and where they came from to slumber forever in this grove of trees and stones. Rarely were the survivors ever there, but their trails of love were: the petrified jack-o-lantern, the heart shaped box of frozen candy, a race car model, a withered American flag, a stuffed Easter bunny, a bucket full of plastic flowers, some withered New Year's balloons, a raggedy teddy bear. Survivors came and went like people in an apartment complex, traipsing in and out with tokens for the dead. But no one saw anyone, no one talked, everyone just stared in disbelieve of their own future. We trudged through the loneliest hallways of grief, maybe nodding a head to a lone car or looking away from the newcomers in black.

I have found great deception in graveyards. My swarthy, aimless rides to my mother's grave, in search of consolation, always left me feeling blank, confused, etched out altogether. On the first Christmas after her death, I ended up at her grave just at dusk, not a soul to be found, not a tear to be shed but this impounding, reckless desolation that ripped away at everything I thought was right. I didn't even get out of the car; I knew she wasn't there. So, instead, I drove to Walgreens, of all places, and bought a hoard of things I didn't need. A sister did likewise just days after, rummaged through her trunk to find a shovel to remove the snow, ended up falling on her knee then wept on the icy ground alongside her stone. Her son wanted to go for help, but there really isn't any. Not in a graveyard, not among the withering flesh of the dead.

What I took back from the graveyard is not what I went to get. The tiniest part of my young heart thought that a visit to her marker would be the missing link but connection is the easiest thing to relinquish in a land of stones and the disparity between hope and despair grows like a weed in an already tangled heart. It has easily been over a decade since I have visited her place in the earth, but I feel her spirit move slowly within me. Like a tree growing over the years, she shapes another ring of time around the center of my being.

Winter Song

My father was different the Christmas two years after she passed; he was very, very different. He stayed longer than he ever had before, didn't rush home but stayed to wash and dry the dishes, stacked them neatly on the counter, careful not to chip the fine glass. He was silent while we busied ourselves with gifts, piling plates with seconds, throwing more dirty dishes into the sink. Methodically, he washed those dishes: each fork, knife, glass, and plate. From time to time, he wiped a hand on his pants then reached up to adjust his hearing aid, maybe trying, I don't know, to tune us out or in or to make the noise of his family a muffled buzz or to pick up on sounds that no one else could hear.

We called to him as we laughed loudly at old home movies. We called to him to come in and relive all the picnics and first communions, to roar with us from our bellies at how thick wasted and klutzy a fourteen-year-old could be. We called to him, but he didn't answer, did not even look up from the sink. Even our piercing shrieks and loud voices teasing and howling at our quirky expressions did not jar him out of his world, did not even turn his head to look but stayed in the presence of himself, nodding and biding to his own thoughts. He looked straight ahead through the curtains out the window, grandchildren tearing about at his feet, fighting and crying over broken toys. He stayed clear of the commotion, moved up close to the sink when someone needed to pass behind, gave glasses of water to the little ones and stayed and stayed and stayed that night but was never really there.

Christmas came and went but that winter never did. I will remember that winter above all. It was the winter of white puppies, the winter of a backfiring tailpipe, the winter of loss and of gain. The winter of jingling keys and the sound of pain. The winter of wishing, the winter of wanting. The winter of her no return. The winter of wanting everyone who passed by my door to be someone else. The winter of running and waiting of want and desire. The churchless winter, the winter filled with God. The winter of lipstick and grey eyes of missing of longing and wanting. The winter of shadows and headlights, of voices and footsteps. It was the winter of passing, the winter of spring, the winter after the winter after the winter when I would leave my husband, the winter when time would fly over me again like a great white swan with huge, blue, sparkling eyes.

Father's Day

I caught my father teetering on a wobbly chair at the top of the basement stairs trying to plug in a small space fan. His grease-stained pants were falling down, hair messy and long, bangs hanging over his glasses. "You're early. Gonna go take a quick bath." "Here let me get that," I offered. I moved the fan near a lower outlet, and he sat down disappointed that I brought ice cream cake instead of apple pie. "That must have set you back about 10 -12 bucks I bet. Go ahead sit down. Yeah. Mama used to like the fan on the floor." As I sat down, my new lab pup collapsed in the heat, frog style, in front of the fan, her chubby belly lifting and lowering her body in an immediate puppy dream while we exchanged small talk.

"Looks like you're making a new walkway," the patio bricks scattered haphazardly on the grass in temporary but permanent positions because he refused our help yet couldn't do it alone; and even if we did come, my sisters and I, to build his walkway some Sunday afternoon, it wouldn't matter; it would still be a long lone walkway out to the alley in its own weedy melancholies. The alley wear I used to hunt for agates, licking the sand off the rocks to disclose their radiant layers. The alley way where he parked his milk truck and surprised us with a kitten someone gave him on his route. The alley where my sister's science experiment mouse perished beneath the trash can.

"Boy, she knows how to relax, just look at her. How many dogs you got now?" Then shook his head with the news of two dogs and four cats. "They're smart old things, just look at her now; she knows what feels good. She's got it made." I mentioned the book *Nop's Trials,* narrated by a kidnapped retriever who ripped your heart out you said, the book we both read years ago, the book that ripped our hearts out. "I just stick to Reader's Digest nowadays," then looked down.

It was only a few months ago that he was still driving hungrily to the library for his weekly stack he would pile on his nightstand. He borrowed a cigarette and looked at the secondhand polo shirts I bought for him. "Yeah, I'll wear these. Boy, I go through shirts fast. Yeah, I can use more like these; hell, I'll put one on after my bath." And I knew that he would and button the collar all the way to the top.

With every visit, I learned more about his tender terms of survival: refrigerator empty except for grape jam, wheat bread, Shasta ginger ale, and boiled ham in a thin plastic bag. He would ask if I was hungry. I never was but felt like I should have been. With his glasses slid halfway down his nose, he justified the empty icebox explaining that he ate mostly at McDonald's, especially breakfast for their coffee and the newspaper he'd swipe claiming they would never miss it. While he brewed raspberry tea, I glanced over the contents of his kitchen table: crossword puzzle, each box filled in with pencil; bolts and screws; odds and ends; the employment section with jobs circled for no one he really knew.

By the telephone was a note from the neighbor: "Jack, if you need anything, anytime, call Hugh." I looked out the window only to see Hugh Potter out putzing in his driveway. I wondered how my dad would make it through another winter. How would he make his morning outings to McDonald's for coffee and the paper, to Walgreens for toilette paper, to the Goodwill for tan work pants? "You know, Dad, you can always come and stay with us." "Nah, I'll be alright." Then he looked down. I thought about him passing out on the kitchen floor the winter before or when he fell in the yard spraining his ankle and breaking his glasses, his wobbly little glasses that half the time were broken and taped together with masking tape.

"Well, Baby, I'm gonna jump in the tub now, put on one of those shirts, maybe kick around for a while, then listen to the ballgame." "Call me, Dad, if you need help. I can clean things up a bit." "Nah, nah, I'm alright." "Well, I love you." "Yeah, yeah, I know. You take most of that cake home now. Go right home to the boys with it. They'll like that," but I didn't want to go home. I just wanted to drive: down the street, through the church parking lot, over the bridge, under the bridge, alongside the bending river letting the ice cream cake melt into a huge puddle on the floorboard of my car.

23

With or Without an *E*

The day's projected forecast was 100 degrees with humidity to match. My father finally called asking for some help. His voice faint and shaken, "Can you take me out to one of those places?" "You want an air conditioner, Daddy?" "Yeah, yeah." "Okay, all right I'm on my way."

When I pulled up to his house, he was walking with tiny, feeble steps down the front stairs. I helped him get situated into the car and as we drove, he gazed out the window looking and wondering like a child. I realized that was the first time in a long time that he was riding as a passenger and traveling much further beyond his five-mile radius. I looked down at his tattered, second-hand shoes, so surrendered and collapsed and listened as he breathed hard, sighing slow indelible sighs.

"You know where this place is?" "Yep, I've been there before. It's tucked up off the frontage road." Walking just slightly in front of me, he grabbed at the entrance walls, then I took his arm to balance him. At once the central air perked him up in total wonder as we walked down the rows and rows of merchandise. With the help of a salesclerk, we picked a unit immediately, the last one that would fit in his bedroom window. Anxious and uneasy, he started to write the check out. I tapped him on the shoulder, "We need to go up front to pay." I turn to ask the clerk a few questions, and he began to write the check again. "We have to wait until we get to the register so they can figure in tax." He looked at me bewildered, and I tried to see clearly to the truest point of his fading eyes, I point, "Up front." At the cashier, I watched him try to finish the check and my heart panged as I saw him write, his shaky innocent handwriting and thought of how he always spelled my name with an "e" and I never had the heart to tell him. It's Ann without an *e*. And when he would say my name, it was always "Aaannne" holding the *A* and *N* for two beats longer. He handed me the pen so I could fill in the amount.

While we drove, I asked, "Is there anywhere else you need to stop?" "Yeah, how about a bite to eat? You like McDonald's, don't you?" In the parking lot, a lady acquaintance stopped and asked about his welfare, helped to steady him, and said that she was glad to see that he wasn't trying to drive himself anymore. He responded with the most regard he could muster in such heat. We sat at McDonald's for a long, long time without saying too much at all. I somehow managed to get the unit into his window, then two days later I called but he didn't know what day it was. He had slept for two days straight in his air-conditioned bedroom. A week later he stroked, never to write or say my name again with or without an *E*.

The Sun is an Easy Circle

I was eighteen when I moved to Oklahoma, terrified when I saw my first tarantula crawl across the lawn. I moved as close to the creature as I could and stood over it in wonder, thinking it was much too large and hairy to be considered a spider. In the morning I would scan the grass quickly hoping to see a little black fluff making its way through the grass and weeds. Often when on the road, I could spot a family of them marching across the Turner Turnpike. I seemed to stick out in Oklahoma like a tarantula on the grass. With my Minnesota accent, expressions, and ways, I never blended in the way I wanted to, though I tried. I tried to move more slowly and tried to say, "Y'all," but it just didn't work. I found a part-time job waiting tables at a restaurant in Tulsa, and often customers asked if I was from Sweden or Switzerland. "No, just St. Paul." "Ah, a Yankee," they'd remark. I wore authentic, leather clogs that I had bought from a store on Grand Avenue before I left. I liked those clogs; they were comfortable. But the manager found humor in calling me the "clog woman" as though I was from another planet. I stopped wearing my clogs and instead wore uncomfortable shoes that left my feet with huge, water blisters. After a work shift, I'd limp to the car and drive home barefoot, sometimes crying. I decided to wear my clogs once more only to trip over a step, sending the platter of chips and salsa whirling through the air leaving me covered with spicy hot sauce. I quit that day and never went back.

The Land

I remember the locusts the best. I remember their huge noise moving up off the trees then hovering in the air. Their eternal clicking subsided only during a rainstorm when they clung to the undersides of leaves. It seemed that even in winter, I could still hear an echo of their constant song. A locust the size of my middle finger clung to the post on my front porch one time. I stepped closer to examine its rock shell. I thought of John the Baptist eating locusts dipped in honey and remembered the time when I was four or five and came close to eating a June bug thinking it was a black jellybean on the sidewalk. I picked the bug up and brought it close to my mouth until I saw its little legs wiggle. I flung it through the air, wiped my mouth, and spit on the grass. Embarrassed that a bug touched my lips, I told no one and after that, ate only what was wrapped. I miss the locusts now. I miss their circling sound, their musical round, their endurance. I depended on them to always be there making noise in a silence I could not bear.

Pumping units and drilling rigs dot an Oklahoma landscape. At night the oil refineries light up the sky like hundreds of tiny Emerald Cities. The constant, "Thud kafoomp, thud kafoomp," of wells being pumped is the heartbeat of the South. Black blood surges through the veins of all oil towns big and small. Compressing unit, drill bit, derrick, field hand, and drilling rig are all terms I became acquainted with as I listened in awe to the depths of the wells and to horror stories of men falling to their deaths.

I don't recall seeing any butterflies in Oklahoma. It seemed too hot for their frail, tissue-paper wings. Southern heat rises up off the asphalt in squiggly vapors like steam from a hot cup of coffee. The only choice when you step into the sun is to drink the heat in great gulps. By the end of June, the grass is brittle hair after a cheap permanent wave, beyond conditioning, beyond repair, fried from root to end. When it does rain, the earth devours the water like a marathon runner letting the moisture spill and slop down her neck

The first summer I lived in Oklahoma a great drought burnt the land. For thirty consecutive days the temperature skyrocketed into the hundreds. The electronic temperature reading at the bank blinked 115 degrees or more for 18 days straight. On those afternoons, I had to ask myself why I ever moved away from Minnesota. Sometimes even the nights wouldn't cool below one hundred. Once the thermometer reaches 110, nothing else seemed to matter. Just like a Minnesota winter dropping to minus 19, what difference does it really make? Minus 19 or minus 22 who can tell the difference? In the heat, the people functioned with an absence of energy moving slowly like ants whose homes had just been destroyed. I vowed to myself that I would never move that slowly.

I was proud of my northern quickness and beamed inside when people asked me to repeat myself when I spoke too quickly. But the heat got the best of me, and I began to move so slowly that I didn't like myself anymore. I stopped curling my hair and stopped wearing makeup; I just let vanity go. My ex-husband and I were unfortunate enough not to have air conditioning but just an attic fan that sucked up what heat it could, so the only relief was an icy bath. I took so many baths that the words printed on the bathtub drain haunted my mind: "Stainless Steel—Push in, Pull out." I would wake each morning with those words on my mind. And after a bath, I just went to sit on that hot, wool blend, scratchy upholstered couch that seemed to bother no one but me. When I asked, "God, aren't you hot?" My ex-father-in-law would calmly look up from the newspaper, "Yea, Sugar, it's a hot one; just sit still now, and you'll get used to it," with beads of sweat dripping from his nose. Any kind of restful sleep was cherished just for winter. A breeze, many nights, was like air from a hair dryer. I used to wet wash rags and place them on my neck and chest desperate for something cool. In the city, the radio stations played *Jingle Bells*, and people murdered each other out of a hot insanity.

Winters in Oklahoma are like Minnesota springs: freezing rain, dreary, biting wind chills. Southern ice storms are magnificent. Every bit of the outside world is glazed with ice, and the whole earth clicks and clacks and slips over upon itself. When great branches break from the weight of the ice, the sound is that of war up over the hill. I tried to keep my composure; I didn't want to let them know of my awe for these ice storms. I wanted them to think that I had seen ice move in such a way, but I really had seen only the wonders of the snow. When I tried to tell them of snowstorms that bury cars, the storms that take the world three days to dig themselves out of, and that people, yes, do actually go about business when it's thirty below, no one wanted to believe me but just said, "Awe, come on now, Hon, is that really so?" After a while, I just stopped talking about Minnesota. It snowed only once during the three years I lived in Oklahoma. It snowed three inches and every school was shut down. I joined the gang for a snowball fight and snowman-making. But the snow didn't seem real to me; it was a tease, a fake, a lie that pulled at my heart. The snowman only lived a day, and I wanted to brag about the snowmen I knew as a child that lived to be four or five months old; I wanted to tell them of Lake Superior waves freezing mightily in midflight. I wanted to tell them of the ice-skating rinks on every block and breeze around skating backward for all of them to see. I wanted them to "ooh" and "aah" and stand in envy of my northern lover. I wanted them to tell me that I should be homesick from the smell of the snow. But it was something they could not do; they had their own lover, their own romance with a land.

Stroud

From Tulsa, we moved to Stroud, a small town of three thousand between Oklahoma City and Tulsa on the Turner Turnpike. "Stroud Proud" or "Stroud America," they called it, a typical small town, if there is such a thing, complete with a grocery store, bank, gas station, convenience stores on every block, a laundromat, friendly people, and gossip. It didn't take long for the news to spread that "the youngest Dixon boy" "got himself a Yankee virgin." My ex-husband, in those days, was a young, wild, beer-drinking, lady's man and from what I was told, "needed some taming." "She's a keeper, Son. Ya better hang on to this one." I remember the first time I met my husband's father at Bob-n-Dots cafe on Main, "She's a mighty sweet little thing. Ya oughta be doing some serious thinking now here, Boy." My ex-husband's reply was, "Yea, Pop, I hear ya."

One particular older man took grandly to my Minnesota ways. He had a deep southern drawl, a handsome rugged face, a teasing, friendly way about him, and a badly deformed hand caused years ago by a serious truck wreck. He always got an enormous charge out of spotting me in a restaurant or the grocery store and bellowing out loudly, "Well, thar's that ole Yankee!" Then making his way towards me in a laughing sort of stride, he'd pat me roughly on the back or give me a push on the shoulder not at all self-conscious of his lame hand. And every time he saw me, not missing it once, he said, "Yea, little gal, I was up once in your neck of the woods, drove through a nasty ole Minnesota blizzard; I just barely made it out of there." Then he would look at me almost fondly as though I had some kind of endurance, shake his head, and say, "I don't know how you northerners get by up yonder."

It seemed that everybody called me, Hon. "What can I getcha, Hon?" "Need some help thar, Hon?" "That's a nice sundress, thar, Hon." Total strangers waved to me, and everybody waved to everybody. If they passed a car on a lonesome dirt road, both drivers waved. If one needed help, someone stopped. If no one needed help, they might stop anyway just to chat. Best known for yacking sessions were the men. In the mornings the Old Rock Cafe was filled with men drinking coffee. Cup after cup, B.S. after B.S. The men would strike up lengthy conversations anywhere, anytime, in the church parking lot, at the gas station at Western Auto, you name it. My ex-mother-in-law chuckled that she just learned to bring a book along so she could at least read while her husband shot the breeze.

In Stroud, we lived at the Rocking-R-Ranch. It wasn't really a ranch but a huge, one-story brick house that was left vacant for years. It was set out in a field overlooking a pond and could be seen from the turnpike exit. This is where I saw my first tarantula, where I learned how to shoot a twelve-gauge shotgun, where I killed scorpions with a broom, where I trot line fished for catfish, where I listened to telltale story after story of Lake Keystone catfish as long as the bed of a pickup truck, and where I looked, for the first time in my life, a cow straight in the eyes.

A herd of cattle grazed our yard in the morning, they came making little need for mowing. In the mornings, the cows came close to the house, within feet of our open, screenless window. On summer mornings they "moooooed" us awake way too early, but I liked having them near. They were sad, dusty cows, and I would have liked to have sprayed them down with the hose. I knew nothing of cows, only of Daisy the cow I painted with watercolor in fourth grade and was pleased with myself for capturing her udders so realistically with the detailed stroke of my brush. But I had never seen one up close with their huge, sorrowful eyes and clunky ways.

Children capture what adults chase after. For little people, the sky is a simple inch of light blue crayon at the top of the page, and the sun is an easy circle with skinny spokes for rays. Every child can draw the sun. And if animals and people get too complicated, their heads too big or small leaving no room on the page for the body, a child can add a stick or two for the arms and legs coming right out of the head, and the teacher will say that it is good. The cows that grazed our land were not like Daisy. Daisy was a happy cow with a bow in her hair and a smile on her face. The round, dark eyes of the cattle in my life only told me of their discomfort in the heat. They moved slowly, barely making room for any car on the road. I felt guilty for honking them out of my path. I did take snapshots of the cows, of their long and grumpy faces. They seemed to almost pose for me. As I walked kindly towards them with my camera, they said to me, I know they did, "Remember us."

The Family Reunion

Annually on the Fourth of July, we attended the family reunion in Maud, Oklahoma. The temperature was inevitably one hundred degrees or more, and if there was a cloud in sight, the sun would not dare to move behind it. Taco salads, instant iced tea, Mexican casseroles, cornbread, okra, banana pudding, peach cobbler; it was the same food and the same flies every year. It was the same rough water fight and the same swim at the public pool and the same volleyball game with the brothers hogging the ball year after year. I tried to have fun at the family reunions. I tried to play volleyball with the others, who seemed to ignore the sweat dripping down their necks, the blue spots floating in the air before their eyes, the strong smell of perspiration, and the scratchy, burnt ground to break a fall. Always in the shade were the older folks cheering and rooting us on to dehydration. I could only take so much and usually slipped away to the air-conditioned house to page through volume after gigantic volume of family photos.

Here we have a picture of my ex-husband and his brothers with their hippy hair and hip-hugging bell bottoms trying to look tough. Here is an old girlfriend not looking very happy at all. And here is a snapshot of my ex-mother-in-law and her sisters twenty-some years ago with their hair teased a foot high, in their swimsuits with the ridiculous flap thing. Here are Aunt Emma and Uncle Fatty. Good old Emma was the one who always lovingly forced me to sample every hot and heavy southern casserole when, in that heat, all I cared for was a salad. In this picture, Fatty is sitting on a lawn chair with a cardboard crown on his head and a large stick in his hand. I never understood that picture, what game they were playing, and why every relative had a copy of that picture in their own album. Fatty was just that, round like a cupid with an expression so happy he almost looked as though he was on the verge of tears. He liked to tease me and give me a hard time about being a Yankee. "I like to get that ole gal's goat, ya know, she's too cotton pickin' serious," I heard him whisper one time to my x. Though, when in the mood, I got him back just fine. Here is a picture of Papaw Patterson, so very different from his brother Fatty. Papaw was crabby, didn't take to these ole reunions too well. He stayed on the outside most of the time, battled with his health, and seemed thirty years older than his younger brother. Papaw was one of the best millwrights in the country. He answered complicated, mechanical questions in his sleep to men outside his bedroom window. Papaw, or "Budster" they called him, grew his own jalapeno peppers in his garden, because no one else could make them hot enough. Here he is with Mamaw, weakly, his arm is around her. They both seem to look unhappy. Papaw always hugged me and made me feel at home. At eighteen, I remember wishing that he was my real grandfather.

Here is a photo of Duke, my ex-husband's oldest brother who was murdered in Pampa, the same day I made Oklahoma my home. Awkward in that time of mourning, I served to keep the children occupied. Still intrigued with my northern accent, they clustered about me, sat on my lap, braided my hair, and touched my arms and earrings. As I sat with them, I could hear Duke's father stumble with weeping and with great moans of pain fall against the walls of the porch. My body stiffened and the children became silent. Duke was quite husky and masculine, divorced and remarried a woman that no one approved of, "sowed his share of oats," his father explained. I examine his picture for some new knowledge of my ex-husband. His mother approaches silently from behind. She touches my shoulder softly and speaks proudly of Duke drinking a gallon of milk a day and of how he always wanted children. He was the only grandson who could dare to compete with Papaw in a pepper-eating contest.

And here is even a picture of me at my first official family reunion just seven days after Duke's death. With my hand, I notice that I am blocking the sun from my eyes. My ex-husband is leaning on me entirely. I am crouching from the weight of his body, and the expression on my face is one I've never seen before.

Now I can hear the others outside laughing and screaming. The thirteenth game of volleyball has begun. As I leave the house, the heat overwhelms me, and the reality of the day sets me back. I stand near the house and watch the play. A cousin hollers up to me, "Come on, Ann! What's wrong? Are you not like us?" They, too, have noticed the difference. I admired them for the way they loved themselves, the way they accept the burnt offerings of their land.

My Loneliness

This is what I have saved for last. I have stepped out to define what I felt, to label a spirit that I can feel at any moment with the smell of heat on 90-degree day. My loneliness there at that time was the same kind of desolation I felt as a child when the sound of the Art Linkletter Show told me it was time for my nap. I can taste that feeling in a half-pint carton of milk or the smell of hot lunch in an elementary school. Tomato Soup and grilled cheese can bring it back or the names of Casey Jones and Roundhouse Rodney.

There was a particular point in Oklahoma where my loneliness seemed more than I could bear. It was on Halloween; we were living in Crescent, Oklahoma next door to the Happy Foods convenience store. It was a corner busy with cars and people. We had no plans and few trick-or-treaters. Something inside of me broke. I called my sister long distance sobbing into the phone. She told me to go to the store and buy myself a package of gum. I was relieved, not for her solution but that she had one at all. We laugh about it now, but there are no measures too small to take for the heart. We do what we can to keep it afloat. I did what I could with a loneliness that shouted back at me when I asked it to leave, a loneliness that moved within my mind as only a lover can and will.

Gigantic Dreams of Okra

I wish we could be something like starfish, living without for only so long, growing back what we lost along the way. If only one little piece of us remained, we could grow ourselves back again into whole new creatures just living by the sea.

I married first, quite young, in my teens to a man, as you know, from Oklahoma, a good man, a kind man. He used to buy me sour apple bubble gum at the gas station every night on his way home from work. I'd blow big, green bubbles while I cooked dinner, wore an apron, and sang show tunes. He would kiss me on the cheek as he set his lunch box on the counter, then would walk out to the garden. I'd watch him sometimes from the window above the sink knowing about those dreams that would go on inside his head. If he had just a few plants, he dreamed them a farm, a shack a mansion, and nothing less. I had trouble sleeping enough to catch him in his dreams, but I liked the way he looked out there, walking slowly with his head down thinking big, important things. I was eighteen; he was twenty-four.

I wrote poetry for him, short, simple poems that I decorated with magic markers. He would kiss me on the cheek, then set them on the dining room table. I stored them for him in a shoe box while he took a bath. I used to page through local cookbooks from the Legion or the church bazaar that his mother had given me, tried my hand at making Maud Shirley's "Angel Fluff Banana Cake" or Martha Strousberg's "Zesty Okra Tubule Salad." With my hair tied back in a bandanna, I would call out to see if he was pleased with what I had made. Always he was, even if he wasn't. I was nineteen on that football Sunday afternoon when I stood up from the couch and declared that I was bored. There was no solution for a city girl in a small southern town so I tried canning: okra, peaches, green beans. I strung bushels of beans on the porch but would never admit to anyone that I was restless. While no one was looking, I would throw handfuls of beans into the bowl without pulling off that stupid string. I never really read the recipes, put too much salt in the beans and not enough vinegar in the pickles. And then there were those wild plum preserves. I never sealed the lids on tight and never figured out how to melt the paraffin, so I served him plum jam on his toast for two weeks straight to use it all up before spoiling. I never told him that I did canning all wrong, didn't even sterilize any of the jars, but his father said, "Them are mighty good pickles."

Lonely and discontent, I drove around town in his black Cutlass, with plastic taped up in one window, wondering what to do. One time I drove 750 miles back home, thinking maybe a change of scenery, the city lights, and the Minnesota landscape would dilute my loneliness, but something always drew me back to the south. When I graduated, we moved to Minnesota where we belonged to a small charismatic church, but over time our growing pains and differences in belief caused us unrest and to eventually go our own ways. During the years after we parted, my memory could easily transport me to that great southern heat, me sitting on top of the kitchen counter in that old, condemned house in Stroud that we cleaned up for free rent. I am there fighting ugly orange contact paper with pieces of it stuck to my hair and arms, crumpling up huge piece after piece. I could hear his semi rumble down our tiny street, and I could still feel my legs running out the door to ride in his semi on a run to Oklahoma City.

As a 26-year-old divorcee, the drought of not seeing him was enough, yet sometimes, in my dreams, he would pour on me. In my dreams, I was with his family on Christmas. No one liked me. I would wake up sad. I dreamt of him driving in the car ahead of me, stopping at the intersection then turning to press his lips against a woman's cheek, arms resting on the back of her seat. I would almost rear-end him, then break myself awake. Or I would dream of running down a hill in his backyard at night. I would cut through his house, sneak into the kitchen, and peek around the corner to see him sitting in a recliner watching television just like his dad. A woman would be running her bath, and I would dart out the front door. Dreaming, I would see him with his girlfriend, nude running towards him on the beach. I'd hide behind a cliff, always seeing the back of her long curly black hair.

I seemed to have been behind him so much in my dreams. Even at church, I was always a few rows back. He was somewhere near the front with one hand in the air before God. I would wake up feeling guilty and far away from something, but it really wasn't God. Sometimes they would come for three nights in a row, maybe two dreams in one sleep, and stayed with me for hours. So why remember any of them? The silence inside after the dream ends, before the story begins is not enough to write these words, the words we don't consider in the gullies of things we find so hard to admit. I admitted that everything I had left for him was subconscious, came out in unexpected sarcasm when I would hear of his plans to remarry, came out in contented laughter when I saw he had painted our house such an unsuccessful blue.

Yet this is where writing falls short when telling the story isn't enough. It leaves me to resort to the romantic when I used to imagine running into him at Target: I imagined seeing him then dodging behind a display to spy. With arms tan and strong, he would look more like his dad with a rounder nose and deepened wrinkles. I would imagine him with a tall, slender girl, almost as tall as he, his daughter perhaps, his arm slung over her shoulder as they chatted and laughed. I imagined what they were saying. The girl would stop by a rack of clothes and hold up a short skirt. He would shake his head in disapproval, then they would walk on with his daughter running her hand over the rack of skirts. I would follow. He would turn and start walking my way; I would almost get caught, dart into a side aisle, knock some bundles of yarn out of a woman's arm, apologize, and try to pick them up for her. She would look at me strangely like I was a shoplifter. I would make my way back into the main aisle then continue shopping, glance in a mirror, fluff my hair then head toward the checkout stand, and balance my checkbook as I waited in line.

Then I would feel two hands grab me by the shoulders: "Annie, Annie? It is you. I can tell that walk anywhere. How are you?" A million memories would flood into me before I could even answer. "I'm fine and you?" "Good. I'm just in town for a few days." I would not be listening to him though. With one look at his face, I would be thinking about how he made me take all the photos and remembering that one little snapshot of the two of us at some church Halloween party: a cheerleader and Superman. We kept pawning that silly picture off on the other. I remember it lying on the floor looking at it for a while then asking, "Do you want this?" "No." So he stuffed it in a box of my sweaters anyway. And before I left with that load, I set it on the counter only to find it again packed in with my books, so on the way out the door I set it on the porch windowsill. Then months later, I ran across it with my mittens and scarves. But it's only right that I ended up with it because I've never been very good at letting go.

"That's great. I'm glad things are going well for you." He would look at me intently as though he was reading my mind. "So, how's your writing coming along?" "Pretty good for now," but I don't want to tell him anything else, don't want to give it away that I've already written this scene. I've already met his daughter and have looked at pictures of the new baby and wife and have already wondered if he gets mad at her if she ever wears his underwear to bed, wondering if she's careful enough to wear the old ones.

So, pages took me a seat ahead of him. Though I felt that I might be, I didn't feel any further along. But I saw how handsome he had weathered and that I could still make him laugh that rolling laugh like his father's. For a while, we would reminisce and talk about the shenanigans of our youth: the giant catfish in the bathtub at the old Rocking-R-Ranch, duck hunting, stringing trot lines across the pond, fishing in that inflatable raft we bought with green stamps and named it the *Unsinkable*, all the pumping units he cleaned and painted and showed off to me, the parking lot stripe painter and painting stripes from here to there and everywhere. Then our memories would begin to springboard off one another until we are leaning into each other and downright giggling together there in the middle of the aisle, blocking traffic. Then an angry shopper would purposely bump him with her cart, which would make us laugh all the harder. We would move out of the aisle, and he would prop his foot up on the bottom of the cart as we both caught our breaths; then he'd look at me closely. Uncomfortable with the silence, I would ask about his family. He would ask about mine.

We would talk about the summer of his brother's death, the rage of that grief, and how his mother sent pictures of his tombstone every Memorial Day.

He would be swept away by that time, and I would look at his hair and recall when he got a permanent just before the divorce was final and how that made me feel so sad and sorry for him because it really didn't look that good. Then he would look at me softly and ask about my mother. Then we would talk about where we're both living. "I always thought that you would move back south," then think about the way he used to like to shovel snow, getting up so early to clear the church lot. I would think about our house and coming back to it the first time, noticing how tidy everything was and that he had rearranged the kitchen counter canisters and about how I had to keep going back time after time for my things and how the next time I ever have to leave someone, I'll just be more organized, won't let my things get so entangled with theirs, keep everything that can hurt in a separate drawer.

He would look at me, then at his watch, "It's time to track down my daughter." We'd say our goodbyes, and when I would get into my car and start driving, I wouldn't know where I was or where I was going. But I would circle around, and end up on the page: I was twenty-nine, nothing like a starfish, but these things would make me think of him: shirtless semi-drivers, lighting cigarettes in the wind, rain in September, the smell of marijuana, packed away poems, loving and leaving, pushing and pulling, lumber yards and contact paper, God in different boxes, climbing trees for mistletoe, sometimes fear, sometimes not, a form of guilt and shame, parking lot stripes and lipstick kisses on dogs, pot roast and pie, T. V. trays, and chicken. These things will never leave me: being a woman, loving a man, waking, resting, sleeping, and dreaming such gigantic dreams of okra.

Time Keepers

My mother use to collect antique eighteen-jewel Swiss watches. She discovered that the more she wore them, the better they ran, so she wore them round the clock, sometimes three or four at a time. When she passed the nurse handed me a plastic bag with three watches in it and said, "Your mother was wearing three watches." I could tell by the curious look on her face that she thought that to be so odd. But it was just my mother, collector of all things, fixer of things that didn't work, master of old things and things that are fragile.

In the basement, she re-furbished enormous antique hutches, frames, mirrors, chairs, and the like with really no caution for the fumes. At any given moment, the house smelled of turpentine, paint remover, and linseed oil. But even more than that, it smelled of imagination and whimsey. She moved within her creativity as any artist does, moving from one idea to the next in a restless attempt at beauty: sewing curtains, slipcovers, pillows; stringing beads; hanging art, moving it and hanging it again; and rearranging furniture. It seemed that every week the French Provincial sofa was someplace new; one time she even put it in the kitchen. But mostly for me, the house smelled of love: on Sundays, pot roast and potatoes after church on the long harvest table; on Easter fancy dresses and shiny yellow shoes, pictures at the Conservatory; on Christmas, potato chips and French onion dip, and Dad bellowing out "Ho, Ho, Ho," from the bedroom. She checked her lists and checked them twice, she paid the bills, scrubbed the floors, and made us pray. She told us that Jesus was our best friend.

It comes with such ease to remember her as the artist sitting at the kitchen table shining brass broaches or dying leather purses, looking out the window watching the neighbor's dog, saying how she wished they'd let him out of his kennel more because all he does is pace, then reminding me not to feed my dog chocolate for the rare chance of canine heart failure, though she never mentioned her own weakened heart. On a quiet winter morning, she died in her sleep with three watches on her wrist.

My father, on the other hand, always kept the kitchen stove clock set 10 minutes ahead. From the bedroom, he'd call out, "Hey, Baby, what time is it out there?" As a teenager, I sarcastically thought, I don't know? Ten minutes later than it is in there? But over the years, I became accustomed to, reliant on, that psychological cushion of *I've still got time,* keeping me ten minutes ahead of every heartbreak to come, every joy to blossom, every quiet neutral day of life.

My dad or Jack as most people called him was as naturally himself as a person could be, with no pretense, no fluff, no filler. He used socks for gloves, wore the same tan jacket for years, and mowed the grass with a push mower. When she passed, we bought him a microwave for his birthday though he refused it. When he was four, his father passed from pneumonia. For financial reasons, he left school after the eighth grade, and after work used to scale the arch of the Robert Street Bridge. He was the man of the family, making a small wage to help his mom. But he was self-taught and well-read. When my mother's health began to decline, with great bravery, he cared for her. No classroom can teach that. No classroom could have taught my dad how to live in a one-bathroom, three-bedroom house with six women. And he too always wore a wristwatch, not three, just one with a dead battery.

You either love your parents for what they are, or you don't. While we live, we die, and when we die, we live. There is nothing in-between. We are either here, or we are there. And since there is no one here to argue this point. I think my parents loved each other, and their love was very much like a long symphony in which I'll never understand the meaning behind the great and forceful gestures and the restless abundance of song and the cacophony and the sorrow and the accord which finally comes to only those in old companionship. Yes, to only those who've had their fill.

My Dad and I

Here in this photograph, we are young. I am two; he is forty-seven. He seems pleased to be holding me so close, his smile wide and handsome as he holds me tightly with both arms, a firm grip on my ruffled diaper, and a rugged hand on my chubby leg. I look as though I could be gurgling something into his ear. I didn't know then I would grow up to leave his arms. And I didn't know that for some reason, I would grow up, to learn to fear him, to walk close to the wall when we passed in the hall. I do not understand for he never laid a hand on me. From the point of that photograph and moving forward no one told me that our physical closeness would grow more scarcer, or I would have wrapped my arms around his neck. But as it is, they dangle in the air preoccupied with a plastic rattle.

As a teenager in late afternoons, I often peeked in at him in his bedroom sleeping, exhausted from his early morning shift. I stood quietly near the door, barely breathing, wondering at him like a child at the zoo pondering a giant bear in hibernation. I liked to watch him sleep and examine him without his knowing. For moments, I would stand there and feel an unnamed, unidentified feeling, one I only had for him. On his dresser was always a stack of clean boxers and socks, a Sanitary Farm Dairy work cap turned upside down containing loose change, matches, keys, sometimes mints, and a candy bar. I often stole the change if I ever needed cash. Some days, if I needed to borrow the car, I would sneak in for the keys. If he woke, he jerked from his sleep saying "What, what, what do you need?" "I just wanted to know if I could use the car." "Go ahead, go ahead, don't wake me anymore." I left in a scurry so unaware of the sacrifices of his worn-out body, the lonely offices of the business of his love.

To ease his mind of responsibility, he gardened when he could and left me notes to weed and water. Lazy and irritated by the interruption, I would try to get by with as little as I could. The weeds were encroaching, more weeds than plants; I never knew what I was yanking out of the ground. He always seemed to catch me sitting in the dirt pulling at something I thought was a weed when I could hear him shout through the screen, "Hey, don't be pulling that now. It's a tomato." I thought, well it looks like a weed to me. He would stand at the kitchen window and examine me doing a half-slop job of watering, tapping on the screen, "Get those eggplants good now. They're out in the sun; soak 'em good." I wanted to take the hose and spray him right through the screen. I had no compassion that his garden gave him pride. I hated those stupid purple plants and grumbled under my breath that I had better things to do. I failed to see the gleam in his eye when the plants were fully gown, his prize possessions in the middle of the kitchen table for everyone to see. He'd pick one up and stroke its shiny skin, "Pretty nice. Good size, good size, don't ya think?"

After I had grown and moved out, one day my car broke down and he gave me a ride to the university to buy a couple of books. As he drove, he seemed irritated, told me I needed some dependable transportation of my own and shook his head in disgust. I was quiet and felt ashamed. He sensed my helplessness and quickly made amends. "Hey now, Baby, I don't mind givin' ya rides, anytime, don't be afraid to call."

Driving the back roads out to the university, we made it there just fine. He knew the city well from the years of his milk route; yet on the way home, we got lost. I knew something was wrong when we passed several streets we should have turned on, but I kept silent. I didn't want him to think I noticed that he didn't know where he was going. At first, I knew where we were but then we got tangled up in the odd side streets so neither one of us knew where we were. "Well, I'll be damned; I think I got us lost here." "That's okay, Daddy, these streets are kind of a tangle town; I've gotten lost here too." I looked at him, his expression so bewildered, so innocent. He was embarrassed for himself and didn't want to show it, didn't know what to think. "I just don't know what's gotten into me. I'll get us headed back in the right direction." I was uneasy and didn't know what to say; I blurted out, "Well that's all right; we'll just take the scenic route."

There is no earthly photo of us together when I held his hand as he took his last breath, but a daguerreotype etched in silver on my heart. He left exactly to the point with no abstraction. For three and a half approximate days of labored breath and dripping morphine, each breath he took was a colon: saying more is on its way. I fed him water on a sponge stick and his little tongue lapped it up, though his half-way eyes were inexact and his spirit neither here nor there.

Then Eat My Love

I ran into my father once at Super America. It was more like seeing a neighbor than a dad. There was an uncomfortable feeling, and I wondered if he had felt it too. For a moment, I imagined how it would be to kiss every time we met. Some fathers and daughters do, you know. He began to pick out the donuts and cookies he wanted from the bakery, and I began my transaction at the Instant Teller and remembered the times he'd have me ride my banana seat bike to the drug store for candy bars 6 for 25 cents. He'd take five and give me one, but I always thought it was worth it. In a loud voice, so that I could hear, he joked with the lady that his daughter didn't bring over any goodies today, so he'd have to buy something for his sweet tooth. And I laughed to myself because of that tooth we share. As he left the store, he said, "See you down the road, Baby," and I thought of how I wanted to take the time to bake him something. Then I realized, at that very moment, that lemon bars and apple pie were the only way I knew how to say, "I love you." Father, then eat my love, if you must, and dab up the crumbs with your moistened finger.

Packing

Take with you whatever it is you think you will need. Leave nothing behind in boxes or in unopened packages. Take with you the first time a man saw your body and how you lay with him in the dark. Take with you the last kiss if you can find it and the way you hit the dog for barking at the mailman delivering bad news. You will never know when you will need this. Also, pack up and take with you the day your cat was run over; that might come in handy if you ever get attached again. Pack with care the look in your father's eyes when he told you to go home, that it was late, and Mama needed her rest. Use those funny Styrofoam things to pack away the middle of the night when bad news lay beside you, pulled the covers off of you, and left you cold and restless. That box will need to go on bottom. The time you let your friend give you an unsuccessful home permanent is important to keep, in case you ever get the urge to try and change yourself again. Oh, and don't forget to pack all of the lies you've told; their awkward, bizarre shapes are hard to pack, I know, but just find long boxes for them. You might have to use them again sometime.

Pack up and take with you when you lost in your mind what you thought you wanted. You'll have to shift everything around to make room for this; it might make the load uneven, but if you don't take it with you today, you'll be looking for it tomorrow. And all the times you've driven on empty, take that with you, too. The directions for knowing what love is should be tucked away in your suitcase in the pocket where your underwear is supposed to go. The dripping bathroom faucet should come along as well, in case they don't have one at the new place.

Wrap in newspaper the exact minute you realized you didn't know whether you were coming or going. Everyone will need to feel this way, so your new neighbor might want to borrow it sometime. And the blizzard of October 1991, tuck that in beside it. Leave all the putdowns behind; they'll catch up to you soon enough.

Label all discarded love *Fragile*. Rest your arm on it while you drive. The box someone put God in can be left on the church doorstep. Use that plastic stuff with the little bubbles to pack up all of your mistakes. If they get broken, you'll have nothing to go by. The moment you found out what it is that you can lose, should be folded up with the maps. Leave with your sister the one thing that could break you.

The Great North Woods

We really had no business, not one of us being experienced campers, to be so bold as to venture into the deep Great North Woods, the four of us: me, two sisters, and a breastfed infant. No, because we thought it most important to remember the adapter that turns the cigarette lighter into an outlet so we could curl our hair while we camped. And we thought it most important to stop frequently at convenience stores for diet pop and candy. And of utmost importance was to wave to all the rugged construction men and even pretend to be lost so we could flutter our eyelashes and ask for directions. Yes, that's who we were.

By the time we reached the Gunflint Trail, it was one O'clock in the morning. Giddy from exhaustion, we laughed until we cried while we pitched the tent. In the deep, deep dark the trial tent pitch in my sister's living room did us little good. The tent fell down three times before we finally got it securely anchored. Of course, we did all the typical "first time on the Gunflint" activities. We visited the bears at the Sanitation Land Fill, thought one of them was charging, and barreled it back to the car, pushing and shoving and laughing, my legs dangling out the door as my sister sped away. We took pictures posing like real outdoorswomen at the top of Honeymooner's Bluff. We rented a canoe and paddled around for a while in the middle of nowhere. On the way home, we bounced the baby back and forth and talked about how we would all go on diets because of all the junk food we had eaten on our quest into the natural wilderness.

The second time into the woods was on my first honeymoon. We had little money so all we could afford was a cheap single-room motel. We were typical tourists and barely knew each other. I can clearly recall the drag on my heart knowing we would have to go back South. I can remember my head on his lap, crying as we drove further away from the Minnesota border. And I can remember sitting there in the middle of the kitchen floor in Crescent, Oklahoma, sorting through wedding gifts, trying to put away cullenders and salad makers and spice racks and not knowing what to do with my sickness for home. But I don't remember anything that the great trees of the north might have said to me. I just remember dreaming of Thunder Bay's Sleeping Giant.

But the third time into those woods was different. I was with new love - everything seemed loud and clear. The trees boomed their mightiness inside of me as I felt my being whittled down to nothing. I was small and confused that I couldn't pinpoint that feeling of mystery about those woods, which begins just miles South of Ely, Minnesota, where the trees let you see nothing but themselves as they cascade with pomp and splendor for display against the highway. They are like women in a beauty pageant, each one wanting your eye and tally on the ballot. But their mass beauty was too surmountable for counts to be kept. They could only register their mark upon a quiet, ready heart.

With steady surveillance, I observed them, felt overcome and dizzy by their quickness to pass by my window. Like on a ride at the fair, a part of me wished it to end, to see things straight and be on my feet again. But the feeling in my stomach kept me hanging on. Though I tagged it then as loneliness, it was not a familiar sort. It wasn't serenity or solitude but a new communion. As we drove on, my mind drifted to the childhood trips my family took to the North Shore: all of us crammed into that old brown Chevy, sleeping on top of each other, fighting for the pillow, and reaching to the front seat for donuts. I can see my dad fighting the wind to keep that old green and black checkered Irish quilt around his shoulders on the shores of Lake Superior. I can hear their hushed voices as I lay across my mother's lap, talking of bills, taxes, new screen doors, patio bricks, and my sister's new boyfriend. Always pretending that I was sleeping, I heard every word. Or the time we drove to the Canadian border and back again in one day so afraid that our cat would be alone when she had her litter of kittens.

When we finally arrived in Ely, it was gloomy, sad, and silent. Even though it was Saturday, it felt ghostly as after a tornado. It seemed the only time there was the hour before dusk and every day was Sunday. I could not picture it ever being cheery and busy as it must be in July. I couldn't picture it being anything else but what it was for me on that bleak November day. And what was it for me that day? It's so hard to discern, so hard to come back to that place in my mind, that feeling in my heart, that feeling of abandonment and belongingness all at once.

We rented our room, unpacked, and rested a bit. After dinner, we decided to take a midnight ride along the Echo Trail. So, there we were right, quite in the middle of nowhere. I felt my fear and my partner played on it, teased me about Sasquatch and that we were about to run out of gas. I thought about the ghost stories my teenage sisters would tell me: the couple whose car stalled in the deep woods, the boy walking for help, the girl waiting alone. I imagined myself stranded like that, falling asleep in the car, then waking to some madman's face pressed against the window. But it was not the kind of fear that I was afraid of. It was fear of what the stillness might do to me. I was afraid of being changed. I was afraid of all those unfamiliar feelings. I was afraid that the trees might want me there to stay to teach me how to love and see clearly all at once.

What Has Been Left

To start from the beginning would be impossible, so I will start where I am, right now today with the totems I have inherited. I will trace them backwards to see if the shadow they cast is any different than it would be had I started at the beginning. I inherited exactly three thousand, six hundred, and eleven dollars and one cent from the remainder of my parent's house and savings, which was divided by five. The family legally transferred a small, fastidiously certain amount of money into an inheritance account, but the rest had been used to pay the nursing home. With the leftover proceeds, one sister bought new carpet, one flew to Mexico, one saved it, and one I will never be for sure.

My father lived at the care center in a small room shared with men who continually left him for a house, wife, grandchildren, fresh cups of coffee, a yard filled with leaves to be raked, or for death. I visited him weekly. On Sunday nights at 5:00 one or two sisters and I would wheel him over to Pizza Pete's in a small, neglected suburbia mall at the south end of St. Paul, where my father took in new scenery like a dog riding in the back of an old pickup. We caught up on the week's activities and then from time to time commented on what features of my father's face or body our family inherited and then the same for our mother. But the vision of her had far faded so we talked about her often to keep her face forward in our minds, lest it slip away entirely.

We have assumed both my father's and mother's thin calves, which in dark nylons, collected like blades of grass at family weddings or funerals; no matter what the weight or age, or disputes between each sister, our lower legs were in union, looking identical as though we were lined up again for a photo on the front lawn on a particularly warm Easter morning. We are proud of the high cheek bones handed down to us from my mother's mother's mother.

Four of the five sisters have inherited distinct creases between the eyes which deepen, not necessarily with time, but more so with worry. Most of us are actually quite stubborn, or strong willed we like to say, which could be attributed to either parent. At least two of us have inherited the tendency to be overly sentimental and disturbed easily by the suffering in the world.

Sometimes we brought our dad new clothes: sweatpants, socks, and easy loose shirts since that were easy for the attendants to pull on and off, turn, adjust, rearrange, until he was comfortable. And always we were on a small mission to find a pair of those, what we called *old man slippers* the ones that look like shoes but are plastic, so we could simply take a damp towel to wash away old food that had dropped from his spoon. Not that anyone cares and not that we never took him out with lumps of old food on his shoes, but that he pointed to his new slippers and loved a shopping bag filled with items for him. My sister cut his hair every two weeks while he sat mesmerized and serene in his chair feeling her soft hands and comb and clippers graze quietly through his hair and neckline. I am not sure from whom we have inherited these fastidious care taking gestures.

I remember one visit quite clearly. As always, he was pleasantly aroused and content with the action at Pizza Pete's, usually a quiet establishment on a late Sunday afternoon, but the crowd was forming for big screen sports, with neither my sister nor I even recognizing it was the beginning of the World Series. After we finished our beers, his mood turned suddenly, and he began to communicate something beyond his ordinary needs. He pointed back to the way of the nursing home so we proceeded to leave. On the way back, he stopped his chair with his feet which confused us all the more. We continued to wheel him, and when we reached the building and his room, he grabbed at the television which was blaring, and so I thought he wanted it off. He refused to eat his dinner, and his chipper, excited mood from earlier had suddenly dissolved.

It wasn't until I reached home that I realized that the first game of the World Series was on, and it wasn't for an hour or so after did I realize that his only wish was to watch the game. We have inherited a female point of view and a lack of understanding such simple male pleasures. I can still see his face looking around the

55

table at three of his daughters, gleaming with what he thought was a World Series get together, that we had planned it that way to share something with him. But nothing had changed. It was always him alone in the kitchen with a beer and smoke watching sports on drizzly Sunday afternoons, while young women would barrel in and out without a care in the world for ball.

Because of him, I have inherited an ache, a lonesomeness, whenever I drive near that old pub. The aroma of pizza and beer and the chatter of strangers, with the excitement of American sports will be a small of the many reminders of my father and his singular masculinity in a female house.

Road Trip

I'd like to take a road trip down a river named *delight,* under clouds picked one by one, beneath a sky that knows the past, past the house I rented years ago with a crumbled path and a wall that held the story of how my family moved me in and three weeks later out because I thought the house was haunted, and they believed me. I might rent a room with a deer head in the lobby and name the deer, *the other side of things.* In the morning, I will wake to sunlight on my pillow and a cat sprawled in the window with one paw on the bright side of my life. Then on the barren road, I'll find a tiger walking backwards toward the future down a lane named *how could I forget.* I could visit the consignment store where my mother sold antiques and near the dusty storefront, I might run into her ghost. I might ask her all the questions I never thought to ask then tell her how nice it was to see her face at last.

Yes, I'd like to take a road trip to circle back around to the door that I let love in while the barge sings out its song. I might pull over for a picnic with an owl who *hoos* a message to the moon and a hare with droopy ears named *sorrow one* and *sorrow two.* I might take a road trip to the city named *be careful* and spend the night swimming in a pool filled with only air. In the morning when I wake again, I'll be floating on tomorrow. I could drive some more along the river's edge and run into a love who took his life so long ago. I won't ask him why; his reasons will not matter but his eyes will fill with water, floating pieces of the sun. I'll spend the night curled up in a ditch of dusty moonlight while a golden ghost floats over spreading starlight in my hair. The next town that I visit might have no name at all but a lake as clear as yesterday, and I'll spend hours in the sand writing letters never written and watch as they dissolve while the waves pull in and out. I could always drive through mountain valleys and meet angels on their way to pull someone from disaster then rent a truck and pick up loads of memory, find my father's ghost shoveling up his share. His hair is sandy grey and eyes as soft as fur. He might not be aware of who I really am, so I will just remember the sound of heart *is here I am.* I might stop at the market where they sell hours by the pound then make some bread that calls for time then slowly bake the years and bring it to a friend.

Oh, I might take a road trip through a town that caught on fire and find all the pieces that I've lost buried under ash. I could drive along the ocean's edge to a village in the hills and name it *there are brighter days ahead*. In this town is a giant bird larger than a tree, with wings named *how could you* and *I'm sorry that I did*. I'll drive some more and visit a museum where every painting has a door and a window that I'll open once I get inside. I might become a queen or a leopard that can fly or simply a woman knitting a road that goes nowhere. Or I might end up in my mother's kitchen while she holds the plate before me, and my father strokes my hair. I could decide to walk along the burrows of my past and find a lion whose eyes are dark, his tail, a ladder to the sun. I might climb it wrung by wrung and find a brush to paint my way and name the burning portrait *I'll love you 'til the end*. If I tire of walking, I might decide to fly over the houses of my heart where all the roofs are gardens and the sky is lined in gold. I could take a needle and mend the past or sew the clouds together as a quilt to keep me warm. I might get too bold and fly too high leaving what I know and find myself becoming a ring around Neptune. If my wings become too weak, I might decide to swim and meet a whale with pale blue eyes and learn the language of the deep.

Acknowledgements

"A Milkman and His Wife" is forthcoming in *The Amaranth Journal*.

"Waves and Wet Kisses" previously appeared in a shortened poetic version in *Mouth of Summer*, Kelsay Books.

"Chocolates" previously appeared as a prose poem in *Mouth of Summer*, Kelsay Books.

"With or Without an E" previously appeared in *The Pinch*.

"Gigantic Dreams and Okra" previously appeared in *MSU Roadrunner Review*

"Timekeepers" is forthcoming in *Twin Bird Review*.

"My Dad and I" previously appeared in *Fresh Words Magazine*.

"Then Eat My Love" previously appeared as a prose poem in *Mouth of Summer*, Kelsay Books.

"Packing" previously appeared in a shortened poetic version in *Mouth of Summer*, Kelsay Books.

"Road Trip" previously appeared in *The Way Back to Ourselves*.

I would like to thank the following people who have helped me and encouraged me during the process of writing these stories. Had it not been for their steady support and guidance, this work would not have been possible. Without the rich and relevant curriculum and instruction in Hamline's MALS and MFA programs, my writing voice would have never come to its full life.

My writing professors: Deborah Keenan, Patricia Francisco, Jim Moore, Mary Logue, and Lawrence Sutin.

My writer's group: Teresa Boyer, Tracy Youngblom, Kirsten Dierking, Janet Jerve, Marie Rickmeyer, Liz Weir, and Kathy Weihe.

All the wonderful people I met while I lived in Oklahoma. I appreciate their depth of character.

My sisters and my husband.

My parents, Jack and Arline, whose humble way of living humbles me every day.

And finally, thank you to Southern Arizona Press for its generosity, direction, and determination to promote writing by creating and funding beautiful books.

About the Author

Ann Iverson is the author of five poetry collections: *Come Now to the Window* by the Laurel Poetry Collective, *Definite Space* and *Art Lessons* by Holy Cow! Press; *Mouth of Summer* and *No Feeling is Final* by Kelsay Books. She is a graduate of both the MALS and the MFA programs at Hamline University. Her poems have appeared in a wide variety of journals and venues including six features on The Writer's Almanac. Her poem "Plenitude" was set to a choral arrangement by composer Kurt Knecht. She is also the author and illustrator of two children's books. A visual artist as well, she enjoys the integrated relationship between the visual and written image. Her artwork has been featured in several art exhibits as well as in a permanent installation at the University of Minnesota Children's Hospital. She is currently working on her sixth collection of poetry as well as several illustrated children's books.

Previous Works

Come Now to the Window
Definite Space
Art Lessons
Mouth of Summer
Queen Freda and the Dangerous Dragon
Queen Freda to the Rescue in New York City
No Feeling is Final